Anna Sewell's

BLACK BEAUTY

Adapted and Abridged by Alice Thorne

Illustrated by **Pers Crowell**

ISBN: 0-448-02250-8 (Trade Edition)

© 1962, by Grosset & Dunlap, Inc.
All rights reserved under International and Pan-American Copyright Conventions.
Published simultaneously in Canada.   Printed in the United States of America.

GROSSET & DUNLAP • Publishers • **NEW YORK**
1971 PRINTING

My Early Home

THE first place that I can well remember was a large, pleasant meadow with a pond of clear water in it. Some shady trees leaned over it, and rushes and water lilies grew at the deep end. Over the hedge on one side we looked into a plowed field, and on the other we looked over a gate at our master's house, which stood by the roadside. At the top of the meadow was a grove of fir trees, and at the bottom a running brook overhung by a steep bank.

While I was young I lived upon my mother's milk, as I could not eat grass. In the daytime I ran by her side, and at night I lay down close by her. When it was hot, we used to stand by the pond in the shade of the trees, and when it was cold, we had a nice warm shed near the fir trees.

As soon as I was old enough to eat grass, my mother used to go out to work in the daytime and come back in the evening.

There were six young colts in the meadow besides me. I used to run with them, and we had great fun. We used to gallop all together round and round the field, as hard as we could go. Sometimes we had rather rough play, for they would often kick and bite as well as play.

One day, when there was a great deal of kicking, my mother whinnied to me to come to her, and then she said:

7

"I wish you to pay attention to what I'm going to say to you. The colts who live here are very good colts, but they have not learned manners. You have been well bred, and your father has a great name in these parts. Your grandfather won the cup two years at the Newmarket races. Your grandmother had the sweetest temper of any horse I ever knew, and I think you have never seen me kick or bite. I hope you will grow up gentle and good, and never learn bad ways. Do your work with a good will, lift your feet up well when you trot, and *never* kick or bite, even in play."

I have never forgotten my mother's advice. I knew she was a wise old horse, and our master thought a great deal of her. Her name was Duchess, but he often called her Pet.

Our master was a good, kind man. He gave us good food, good lodging, and kind words. We were all fond of him, and my mother loved him very much. When she saw him at the gate, she would neigh for joy and trot up to him. He would pat and stroke her, and then he would give me a piece of bread which was very good, and sometimes he brought a carrot for my mother. All the horses would come to him, but I think we were his favorites.

I was two years old when something happened which I have never forgotten. It was early in the spring. There had been a frost in the night, and a light mist still hung over the meadows. I and the other colts were feeding at the lower part of the field when we heard, off in the distance, the cry of dogs. The oldest of the colts raised his head, pricked up his ears, and said, "There are the hounds!" He immediately cantered off, followed by the rest of us, to the upper part of the field, where we could look over the hedge and see several fields beyond. My mother was standing near and seemed to know all about it.

"They have found a hare," said my mother, "and if they come this way we shall see the hunt."

And soon the dogs were tearing down the field of young wheat next to ours. I never heard such a noise as they made. They did not bark but kept on a "yo! yo-o-o! yo! yo-o-o!" at the top of their voices. After them came a number of men on horseback, some of them in green coats, all galloping as fast as they could. They made straight for our meadow where the high bank and hedge overhang the brook.

"Now we shall see the hare," said my mother, and just then a hare wild with fright rushed by, and made for the trees. On came the dogs. They burst over the bank, leaped the stream, and came dashing across the field, followed by the huntsmen. The hare tried to get through the fence. It was too thick, and she turned sharp around to make for the road, but it was too late. The dogs were upon her with their wild cries. We heard one shriek, and that was the end of her. All the gentlemen seemed well pleased.

As for me, I was so astonished that I did not at first see what was going on by the brook. But when I did look, there was a sad sight. Two fine horses were down, one was struggling in the stream, and the other was groaning on the grass. One of the riders was getting out of the water covered with mud, and the other lay quite still.

"His neck is broken," said my mother.

There was no noise now. Even the dogs were quiet and seemed to know that something was wrong. They carried him to my master's house. I heard afterward that it was young George Gordon, the Squire's only son, a fine, tall young man, and the pride of his family.

Mr. Bond, the horse doctor, came to look at the black horse that lay groaning on the grass. He felt him all over and shook his head. One of the horse's legs was broken. Then someone ran to our master's house and came back with a gun. Presently there was a loud bang and a dreadful shriek, and then all was still. The black horse moved no more.

My mother seemed much troubled. She never would go to that part of the field afterwards. Not many days later, they carried young Gordon to the churchyard to bury him. What they did with the black horse I never knew—but it was all for one poor little hare.

My Breaking In

I WAS now beginning to grow handsome. My coat had grown fine and soft and was bright black. I had one white foot and a pretty white star on my forehead.

When I was four years old, Squire Gordon came to look at me. He examined my eyes, my mouth, and my legs. He seemed to like me and said, "When he has been well broken in, he will do very well." My master said he would break me in himself, as he did not want me to be frightened or hurt, and the next day he began.

Everyone may not know what breaking in is. It means to teach a horse to wear a saddle and bridle and to carry on his back a man, woman, or child—to go just the way they wish, and to go quietly. He must always do his master's will, even though he may be very tired or hungry. But the worst of all is, once his harness is on, he may neither jump for joy nor lie down for weariness. So you see, this breaking in is a big step in training a horse.

At first, I hated it and never felt more like kicking, but of course I could not kick such a good master. At last, one morning my master got on my back and rode me around the meadow on the soft grass. It certainly did feel odd. But I must say I felt rather proud to carry my master, and as he continued to ride me a little every day, I soon became accustomed to it, and in time could do my work as well as my mother.

Early in May, a man came from Squire Gordon's. He took me away to the Hall. My master said, "Good-by—be a good horse, and always do your best." I could not say "good-by," so I put my nose into his hand. He patted me gently, and I left my first home.

Squire Gordon's Park was near the village of Birtwick and was entered by a large iron gate. Then you trotted along on a smooth road, between clumps of large old trees, which brought you to the house and the gardens. Beyond this lay the paddock, the old orchard, and the stables.

The stable into which I was taken was very roomy, with four good stalls. The first stall was a large square one with a wooden gate. The three others were good stalls but not nearly so large as this one. This was called a loose box, because the horse that was put into it was not tied up, but left loose, to do as he liked. It is a great thing to have a loose box.

The groom put me into this fine box. It was clean, sweet, and airy. I never was in a better box than that, and the sides were not too high for me to see all that went on, through the iron rails at the top.

He gave me some very nice oats, he patted me, spoke kindly, and then went away.

When I had eaten my oats, I looked around. In the stall next to mine stood a little fat gray pony with a thick mane and tail, a very pretty head, and a pert little nose.

I put my head up to the iron rails at the top of my box and said, "How do you do? What is your name?"

He turned around, held up his head, and said, "My name is Merry-legs. I am very handsome. I carry the young ladies on my back, and sometimes I take out our mistress in the low cart. They think a great deal of me, and so does James. Are you going to live next door to me in the box?"

I said, "Yes."

"Well, then," he said, "I hope you are good-tempered. I do not like anyone next door who bites."

Just then a horse's head looked over from the stall beyond. The ears were laid back, and the eye looked rather ill-tempered. This was a tall chestnut mare, with a long, handsome neck. She looked across at me and said, "So it is *you* who have turned me out of my box! It is a very strange thing for a colt like you to come and turn a lady out of her own home."

"I beg your pardon," I said. "The man who brought me here put me here, and I had nothing to do with it. And as for being a colt, I am four years old and a grown-up horse. I never had words yet with horse or mare, and it is my wish to live at peace."

"Well," she said, "we shall see. Of course, I do not want to have words with a young thing like you."

In the afternoon, when she went out, Merrylegs told me all about it.

"Ginger has a bad habit of biting and snapping. When she was in the loose box she used to snap very much. One day she bit James in the arm and made it bleed, and so Miss Flora and Miss Jessie were afraid to come into the stable. They used to bring me nice things to eat, an apple or a carrot, or a piece of bread, and I miss them very much. I hope they will now come again, if you do not bite or snap," he finished.

I told him I never bit anything but grass, hay, and corn, and could not think what pleasure Ginger found in it.

"Well, I don't think she does find pleasure," Merrylegs said. "It is just a bad habit. She says no one was ever kind to her, and why should she not bite? I'm sure, if all she says is true, she must have been very badly used before she came here. But John and James do all they can to please her, and our master never uses a whip if a horse acts right. So I think it is all Ginger's fault that she did not stay in that box."

Birtwick Park

THE NEXT morning, John Manly, the coachman, took me into the yard and gave me a good grooming until my coat was soft and bright. After breakfast he came and fitted me with a saddle and bridle. Then he rode me, first slowly, then a trot, then a canter; and when we were on the common he gave me a light touch with his whip, and we had a splendid gallop.

"Ho, ho, my boy!" he said, as he pulled me up. "You would like to follow the hounds, I think."

The next day I was brought up for my master. I tried to do exactly what he wanted me to do. I found that he was a very fine rider, and thoughtful of his horse, too. When we came home, the lady was at the Hall door as he rode up.

"Well, my dear," she said, "how do you like him?"

"A more pleasant creature I never wish to mount," the Squire replied. "What shall we call him?"

"Would you like Ebony?" said she. "He is as black as ebony."

"No, not Ebony."

"Will you call him Blackbird, like your uncle's old horse?"

"No, he is far more handsome than old Blackbird ever was."

"Yes," she said. "He really is a beauty, and he has such a sweet, good-tempered face and such a fine, intelligent eye—what do you say to calling him Black Beauty?"

"Black Beauty—why, yes, I think that is a very good name. If you like, it shall be his name." And so it was.

John, the coachman, seemed very proud of me. He used to make my mane and tail almost as smooth as a lady's hair, and he would talk to me a great deal. Of course I did not understand all he said, but I learned what he wanted me to do. I grew very fond of him.

A few days after this, I had to go out with Ginger in the carriage. I wondered how we would get on together. But except for laying her ears back when I was led up to her, she behaved very well. She did her work honestly and did her full share, and I never wish to have a better partner in double harness.

As for Merrylegs, he and I soon became good friends. He was such a cheerful, plucky, good-tempered little fellow that he was a favorite with everyone, especially with Miss Jessie and Miss Flora, who used to ride him about in the orchard and have fine games with him and their little dog Frisky.

On fine Sundays in the summertime, Ginger and I were turned out into the old orchard. The grass was so cool and soft to our feet, the air so sweet, and the freedom to do as we liked was so pleasant—to gallop, to lie down and roll over on our backs, or to nibble the sweet grass.

One day when Ginger and I were standing alone in the shade, we talked for a long time. She wanted to know all about my bringing up and breaking in, and I told her.

"Well," she said, "if I had had your bringing up, I might have had as good a temper as you, but now I don't believe I ever shall."

"Why not?" I asked.

"Because it has all been so different with me," she replied. "I never had anyone, horse or man, that was kind to me, or that I cared to please. In the first place, I was taken from my mother as soon as I was weaned. There was no kind master to look after me, like yours, and talk to me and bring me nice things to eat. The man that had the care of us never gave me a kind word in my life. Everything he did was rough, and I began to hate him. He wanted to make me afraid of him, but I was too high-mettled for that—and one day when he had aggravated me more than usual, I bit him. So, of course, I was sold.

"The next place," Ginger went on, "was enough to drive one mad. I began to plunge and kick with all my might. I soon broke a lot of harness and kicked myself clear—so that was the end of that place. I came here not long before you did," she added, "but I had then made up my mind that men were my natural enemies and that I must defend myself. Of course, it is very different here, but who knows how long it will last?"

"Well," I said, "I think it would be a real shame if you were to bite or kick John or James."

"I don't mean to," she said, "while they are good to me. I did bite James once pretty sharp, but John said, 'Try her with kindness.' And instead of punishing me as I expected, James came to me with his arm bound up and brought me a bran mash and stroked me. And I have never snapped at him since, and I won't either."

17

A Stormy Day

ONE DAY late in autumn, my master had to go on a long journey. I was put in the dogcart, and John went, too. There had been a great deal of rain, and now the wind was very high and blew the dry leaves across the road in a shower. We went along merrily till we came to the toll bar and the low wooden bridge.

The man at the gate said the river was rising fast, and he feared it would be a bad night. Many of the meadows were under water, and in one low part of the road the water was halfway up to my knees.

When we got to the town, the master's business kept him a long time, and we did not start for home till late in the afternoon. The wind was then much higher, and I heard the master say to John that he had never been out in such a bad storm. We went along the edge of a wood, where the great branches were swaying like twigs, and the rushing sound was terrible.

"It would be most unfortunate," said the master, "if one of these branches came down upon us."

The words were scarcely out of his mouth when there was a groan, and a crack, and a splitting sound. Crashing and tearing down among the other trees came an oak, torn up by the roots, and it fell right across the road just before us.

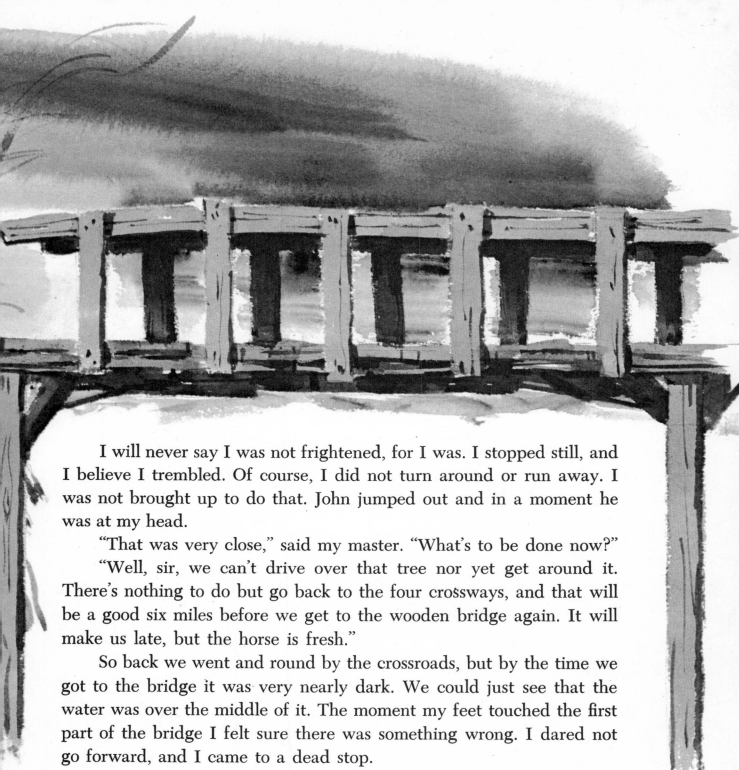

I will never say I was not frightened, for I was. I stopped still, and I believe I trembled. Of course, I did not turn around or run away. I was not brought up to do that. John jumped out and in a moment he was at my head.

"That was very close," said my master. "What's to be done now?"

"Well, sir, we can't drive over that tree nor yet get around it. There's nothing to do but go back to the four crossways, and that will be a good six miles before we get to the wooden bridge again. It will make us late, but the horse is fresh."

So back we went and round by the crossroads, but by the time we got to the bridge it was very nearly dark. We could just see that the water was over the middle of it. The moment my feet touched the first part of the bridge I felt sure there was something wrong. I dared not go forward, and I came to a dead stop.

"Go on, Beauty," said my master, and he gave me a touch with the whip. I jumped, but I dared not go forward.

"There's something wrong, sir," said John, and he sprang out of the dogcart and came to my head and looked all about. He tried to lead me forward. "Come on, Beauty, what's the matter?" Of course, I could not tell him, but I knew very well that the bridge was not safe.

Just then the man at the tollgate on the other side ran out of the house, swinging a lantern.

"Halloo! Stop! Stop!" he cried.

"What's the matter?" shouted my master.

"The bridge is broken in the middle, and part of it was carried away. If you come on, you'll be into the river!"

"Thank God!" said my master.

"You Beauty!" said John, and he took the bridle and gently turned me round to the right-hand road by the riverside. The wind seemed to have lulled after that furious blast that tore up the tree. It grew darker and darker, and very still. I trotted quietly along, the wheels hardly making a sound on the soft road.

At last we came to the Park gates, and found the gardener looking out for us. He said that my mistress had been greatly worried ever since dark, fearing some accident had happened. We saw a light at the Hall door, and as we came up she ran out, saying, "Are you really safe, my dear? Oh, I have been so anxious, imagining all sorts of things. You haven't had an accident?"

"No, my dear. But if your Black Beauty had not been wiser than we were, we would all have been carried down the river at the wooden bridge."

I heard no more as they went into the house, and John took me to the stable. Oh, what a good supper he gave me that night! A good bran mash and some crushed beans with my oats. And such a thick bed of straw! I was glad of it, for I was tired.

The Fire

ONE morning early in December, James was just coming in from the corn chamber with some oats when the master came into the stable. He looked very serious and held an open letter in his hand. John touched his cap and waited for orders.

"Good morning, John," said the master. "I have a letter from Sir Clifford Williams. He wants me to find him a trustworthy young groom, about twenty or twenty-one years old, who knows his business. If James could get the job, it would be a good start for him. How old are you, James?"

"I will be nineteen next May, sir."

"That's young. What do you think, John?"

"Well, sir, it is young. But he is as steady as a man, and is strong and well grown. And though he has not had much experience in driving, he has a light, firm hand and a quick eye, and he is very careful."

A few days after this conversation it was decided that James would go to Clifford Hall in a month. In the meantime, he was to get all the practice in driving that could be given to him. Ginger and I were put into the carriage and James drove us. At first, John rode with him on the box, telling him this and that, and then James drove alone. Not long after this, my master and mistress decided to visit some friends about forty-six miles away, and James was to drive them.

The first day we traveled thirty-two miles. There were some long, heavy hills, but James drove so carefully and thoughtfully that we were not at all distressed. We stopped once or twice on the road, and just as the sun was going down, we reached the town where we were to spend the night. We stopped at the biggest hotel and drove into a long yard, at the farther end of which were the stables. Two hostlers came to take us out. The head hostler unbuckled my harness and led me to a long stable with two or three horses in it. The other man brought Ginger. James stood by while we were rubbed down and cleaned. Then, after Ginger and I had had our corn, James and the head hostler left the stable together.

Later on in the evening, a young man with a pipe in his mouth stopped in at the stable to gossip with the under hostler.

"Just run up the ladder into the loft, will you, Towler," the hostler said, "and put some hay into this horse's rack. Only put down your pipe."

"All right," said the other, and went up through the trap door. James came in later to look at us the last thing, and then the door was locked.

I cannot say how long I slept, but I woke up very uncomfortable, though I hardly knew why. I got up. The air seemed all thick and choking. I heard Ginger coughing, and one of the other horses moved about restlessly. It was quite dark and I could see nothing, but the stable was full of smoke which seemed to be coming from the open trap door. I

heard a soft, rushing sort of noise, and a low crackling and snapping, so strange that it made me tremble all over.

At last I heard steps outside, and the under hostler burst into the stable with a lantern and tried to untie the horses and lead them out. But he seemed so frightened himself that he frightened us still more. None of us would go with him. He tried to drag each of us out by force. Of course that was no use. Then he ran out of the stable.

No doubt we were very foolish, but danger seemed to be all around, and there was nobody we knew to trust, and all was strange and uncertain. The rushing sound grew louder, and as I looked up through the bars of my empty rack I saw a red light flickering on the wall. Then I heard a cry of "Fire!" and the head hostler quietly and quickly came in. He got one horse out and then another, and all the while the flames were playing round the trap door, and the roaring overhead was dreadful.

The next thing I heard was James' voice, quiet and cheery, as it always was. "Come, my beauties, it is time for us to be off, so wake up and come along!" I stood nearest the door, so he came to me first, patting me as he came in.

"Come, Beauty, on with your

bridle, my boy! We'll soon be out of this smother." It was on in no time. Then he took the scarf off his neck and tied it lightly over my eyes. Patting and coaxing, he led me out of the stable. Safe in the yard, he slipped the scarf off my eyes and shouted, "Here, somebody! Take this horse while I go back for the other!"

A tall man stepped forward and took me, and James darted back into the stable. I set up a shrill whinny as I saw him go. There was much confusion in the yard, but I kept my eyes fixed on the stable door, where the smoke poured out thicker than ever, and I could see flashes of red light. Presently I heard a loud, clear voice, which I knew was master's:

"James Howard! James! Are you there?"

There was no answer, but I heard a crash inside the stable, and the next moment I gave a loud, joyful neigh, for I saw James coming through the smoke leading Ginger after him.

"My brave lad!" said master, laying his hand on his shoulder. "Are you hurt?"

James shook his head, for he could not yet speak.

"Aye," said the big man who held me. "He is a brave lad and no mistake about it."

There came a sound of galloping feet and loud, rumbling wheels. "'Tis the fire engine! The fire engine!" shouted two or three voices. "Stand back! Make way!" And clattering and thundering over the stones, two horses dashed into the yard with the heavy engine behind them. The firemen leaped to the ground. There was no need to ask where the fire was—it was leaping up in a great blaze from the roof.

As soon as James and Ginger had got their breaths back, master led us out into the broad, quiet market place. The stars were shining, and except for the noise behind us, all was still. Master took us to a large hotel on the other side. As soon as the hostler came for us, master said, "James, I must now hasten to your mistress. I trust the horses entirely to you. Order whatever you think is needed." And with that he was gone.

The next morning, as the hostler was rubbing me down, I heard him tell James that the fire had been started by the young man named Towler. He had gone up the ladder to put down some hay but had not laid aside his pipe first, as the under hostler had asked him to do. I remember our John Manly's rule, never to allow a pipe in the stable, and thought it ought to be the rule everywhere.

Master came in then to see how we were and to speak to James. I did not hear much, but I could see that James looked very happy, and I thought the master was proud of him.

Going for the Doctor

WE returned home about a week later, and we were glad to be in our own stable again. John was equally glad to see us. Before he and James left us for the night, James said, "I wonder who is coming in my place."

"Little Joe Green," said John.

"Little Joe Green! Why, he's a child!"

"He is fourteen and a half," said John.

"But he is such a little chap!"

"Yes, he is small, but he is quick and willing, and kind-hearted, too, so I said I was willing to try him."

"It will make you a lot of extra work, John," said James.

"Well," said John with a laugh, "work and I are very good friends. I never was afraid of work yet."

"You are a very good man," said James. "I wish I may ever be like you."

The next day Joe came to the stables to learn all he could before James left. Joe was a nice bright little fellow, and always came whistling to his work. James taught him upon Merrylegs, and Merrylegs was a

good deal put out at first to be "mauled about," as he said, "by a boy who knows nothing." But toward the end of the second week he told me confidentially that he thought the boy would turn out well.

At last the day came when James had to leave us. Everyone was sorry to lose him. As for Merrylegs, he pined after him for several days and went quite off his appetite. So John took him out several mornings with a leading rein, when he exercised me. Trotting and galloping by my side got the little fellow's spirits up again, and he was soon all right.

One night, a few days after James had left, I had eaten my hay and was lying down in the straw fast asleep, when I was suddenly wakened by the stable bell ringing very loud. I heard John running up to the Hall. He was back in no time, calling out, "Wake up, Beauty, you must go well now, if ever you did."

Almost before I could think, he had my saddle and bridle on and took me at a quick trot up to the Hall door. The Squire stood there with a lamp in his hand.

"Now, John," he said, "ride for your life, that is, for your mistress' life. There is not a moment to lose. Give this note to Dr. White. Give Beauty a rest at the inn and be back as soon as you can."

John said, "Yes, sir," and was on my back in a minute. The gardener who lived at the lodge had heard the bell ring, and was ready with the gate open, and away we went through the Park and through the village and down the hill.

There was before us a long piece of level road by the riverside. John said to me, "Now, Beauty, do your best." And so I did. I needed no whip nor spur, and for two miles I galloped as fast as I could lay my feet to the ground. When we came to the bridge, John pulled me up a little and patted my neck. "Well done, Beauty, good old fellow!" he said. He would have let me go slower, but my spirit was up, and I was off again as fast as before. We came through a dark wood, then uphill, then downhill, till after an eight-mile run, we came to the town. It was all quite still except the clatter of my feet on the stones.

The church clock struck three as we drew up to Dr. White's door. John knocked at the door like thunder. A window was thrown up, and Dr. White put his head out.

"Mrs. Gordon is very ill, sir," said John. "Master wants you to go there. He thinks she will die if you cannot get there—here is a note."

"Wait," the doctor said. "I will come at once."

He shut the window and was soon at the door. "The worst of it is," he said, "that my horse has been out all day and is worn out. What's to be done? Can I have your horse?"

"He has come at a gallop nearly all the way, sir, and I was to give him a rest here. But I think my master would not be against it if you think fit, sir."

"All right," he said, "I will soon be ready."

John stood by me and stroked my neck. I was very hot. The doctor came out with his riding whip.

"You will not need that, sir," said John. "Black Beauty will go till he drops. Take care of him, sir."

In a minute we had left John far behind. I did my best, and when we came to the hill, the doctor drew me up. "Now, my good fellow," he said, "take some breath." I was glad he did, for I was nearly spent, but that breathing helped me on, and soon we were in the Park. Joe was at the lodge gate. My master was at the Hall door, for he had heard us coming. He spoke not a word. The doctor went into the house with him, and Joe led me to the stable. I was glad to get home, for my legs shook under me and I could only stand and pant.

Poor Joe! He was young and small, and as yet he knew very little. He rubbed my legs and my chest but he did not put my warm cloth on me. He thought I was so hot I would not like it. Then he gave me a pailful of water to drink. It was cold and very good, and I drank it all. Then he gave me some hay and some corn, and thinking he had done right, he went away.

Soon I began to shake and tremble, and turned deadly cold. My legs ached, my loins ached, and my chest ached, and I felt sore all over. Oh, how I wished for my warm thick cloth as I stood and trembled! I wished for John, but he had eight miles to walk, so I lay down on my straw and tried to go to sleep. After a long while, I heard John at the door. I gave a low moan, for I was in great pain. He was at my side in a moment, stooping down by me. I could not tell him how I felt, but he seemed to know it all. He covered me up with three warm cloths, and then ran to the house for warm water. He made me some hot gruel which I drank, and then I think I went to sleep.

John seemed to be put out. I heard him say to himself over and over again, "Stupid boy! Stupid boy! No cloth put on, and I dare say the water was cold, too. Boys are no good!" But Joe was a good boy after all.

I was now very ill. I could not draw my breath without pain. John nursed me night and day. My master, too, often came to see me.

"My poor Beauty," he said one day. "My good horse, you saved your mistress' life." I was very glad to hear that, for it seems the doctor said if we had been a little longer, it would have been too late. John told my master he never saw a horse go so fast in his life—it seemed as

if the horse knew what was the matter. Of course, I did, though John thought not; at least, I knew that John and I must go at the top of our speed, and that it was for the sake of the mistress.

I do not know how long I was ill. Mr. Bond, the horse doctor, came every day. One day he bled me and I felt very faint and thought I would die. I believe they all thought so, too.

One night John had to give me some medicine and Thomas Green came in to help him. I heard Tom Green say in a low voice:

"I wish, John, you'd say a bit of a kind word to Joe. The boy is quite broken-hearted. He says if Beauty dies it will have been all his fault. It goes to my heart to hear him. I think you might give him just a word. He is not a bad boy."

John said slowly, "You must not be too hard on me. I know Joe meant no harm. I never said he did. I know he is not a bad boy; but, you see, that horse is the pride of my heart. And to think that his life may be flung away in this manner is more than I can bear. But if you think I am hard on the boy, I will try to give him a good word tomorrow —that is, I mean, if Beauty is better."

I heard no more of this conversation, for the medicine did well and sent me to sleep, and in the morning I felt much better.

The Parting

I HAD now lived in Birtwick three happy years, but sad changes were about to come over us. We heard from time to time that our mistress was ill. The doctor was often at the house, and the master looked grave and anxious. Then we heard that she must leave her home at once and go to a warm country for two or three years. The news fell upon the household like the tolling of a death bell. The master began at once to make arrangements for breaking up his home and leaving England.

John went about his work silent and sad, and Joe scarcely whistled. The first to go were Miss Jessie and Miss Flora, with their governess. They came to bid us good-by. They hugged Merrylegs like an old friend, and so he was. Then we heard what had been arranged for us.

Master had sold Ginger and me to his old friend, the Earl of W——, for he thought we would have a good place there. He had given Merrylegs to the Vicar, who wanted a pony for Mrs. Blomefield and the children. But it was on condition that Merrylegs never be sold.

Joe was engaged to take care of him and to help in the house, so I thought Merrylegs was well off.

John had offers of several good jobs, but he decided to wait a little and look around.

The evening before they left, the master came into the stable to give his horses a last pat. He seemed very low-spirited; I knew that by his voice. I believe we horses can tell more by the voice than many men can.

Then master thanked John for his long and faithful service, but that was too much for John. "Please don't, sir," he said. "I can't bear it. We shall never forget you, sir, and God willing, we may some day see mistress back again like herself." Master gave John his hand, but he did not speak, and they both left the stable.

The last sad day had come. The footman and the heavy luggage had gone off the day before. There was only master and mistress and her maid. Ginger and I brought the carriage up to the door for the last time.

Master came down the steps with the mistress and placed her carefully in the carriage. (I was on the side next to the house and could see all that went on.) "Good-by again," he said to the house servants who stood around. "We shall not forget any of you." He got in, too, and said, "Drive on, John."

Joe jumped up, and we trotted slowly through the Park and the village. When we reached the railway station, I heard mistress say in her own sweet voice, "Good-by, John, God bless you." I felt the rein twitch, but John made no answer. Perhaps he could not speak.

Poor Joe! He came and stood close to our heads to hide his tears. Very soon the train came puffing up into the station. In two or three minutes the doors were slammed, the guard whistled, and the train glided away in a cloud of white smoke.

When it was quite out of sight, John took the reins, mounted the box, and with Joe drove slowly home, but it was not our home now.

The next morning after breakfast Joe harnessed Merrylegs to take him to the vicarage. He came first and said good-by to us, and Merrylegs neighed to us from the yard. Then John put the saddle on Ginger and the leading rein on me, and rode us across country to Earlshall Park, where the Earl of W—— lived. There was a very fine house and large stables. We went into the yard through a stone gateway, and John asked for Mr. York, the coachman. He was a fine-looking man and his voice said at once that he expected to be obeyed. He called a groom to take us to our boxes and invited John to take some refreshment.

We were taken to a light, airy stable and placed in boxes adjoining each other. Then we were rubbed down and fed. In about half an hour, John and Mr. York came in to see us.

"Now, Mr. Manly," he said, after carefully looking us over, "we all know that horses have their peculiarities as well as men. Is there anything particular about either of these that you would like to mention?"

"I had better mention that we have never used the bearing rein with either of them. The black horse never had one on, and the dealer said it was the gag bit that spoiled the other's temper."

"Well," said York, "if they come here they must wear the bearing rein. I prefer a loose rein myself, and his lordship is always very reasonable about horses. But my lady—that's another thing—she will have style. If her carriage horses are not reined up tight she wouldn't look at them. I always stand out against the gag bit, and shall do so, but it must be tight up when my lady rides!"

"I am sorry for it, very sorry," said John, "but I must go now, or I shall miss the train."

He came round to each of us to pat and speak to us for the last time. His voice sounded very sad.

I held my face close to him. That was all I could do to say good-by. Then he was gone, and I have never seen him since.

A Strike for Liberty

THE NEXT day Lord W—— came to look at us. York then told him what John had said about us.

"Well," said Lord W——, "you must keep an eye to the mare, and put the bearing rein easy. I dare say they will do very well with a little humoring at first. I'll mention it to her ladyship."

In the afternoon we were harnessed and put in the carriage. As the stable clock struck three, we were led round to the front of the house. It was all very grand, but not half so pleasant as Birtwick, if a horse may have an opinion. Two footmen were standing ready, and presently we heard the rustling sound of silk as my lady came down the flight of stone steps. She stepped around to look at us. She was a tall, proud-looking woman, and did not seem pleased about something, but she said nothing and got into the carriage. This was the first time I ever wore a bearing rein. I must say, though it certainly was a nuisance not to be able to get my head down now and then, it did not pull my head higher than I was accustomed to carry it. I felt anxious about Ginger, but she seemed to be quiet and content.

The next day at three o'clock we were again at the door, and the footmen as before. We heard the silk dress rustle, and the lady came down the steps. In an imperious voice she said, "York, you must put those horses' heads higher. They are not fit to be seen."

York got down and said very respectfully, "I beg your pardon, my lady, but these horses have not been reined up for three years. My lord said it would be safer to bring them to it by degrees, but if your ladyship pleases, I can take them up a little more."

"Do so," she said.

York came round to our heads and shortened the rein himself—one hole, I think. But every little makes a difference, and that day we had a steep hill to go up.

Of course I wanted to put my head forward and take the carriage up with a will, as we had been used to do. But no, I had to pull with my head up now, and that took all the spirit out of me, and the strain came on my back and legs.

When we came in, Ginger said, "If they strain me up tight, why, let 'em look out! I can't bear it, and I won't!"

One day my lady came down later than usual, and the silk rustled more than ever.

"Drive to the Duchess of B——'s," she said, and then after a pause, "Are you never going to get those horses' heads up, York? Raise them at once, and let us have no more of this humoring and nonsense."

York came to me first, while the groom stood at Ginger's head. He drew my head back and fixed the rein so tight that it was almost unbearable. Then he went to Ginger, who was impatiently jerking her head up and down against the bit. She had a good idea of what was coming, and the moment York took the rein off the terret in order to shorten it, she took her opportunity and reared up so suddenly that York had his nose roughly hit and his hat knocked off. The groom was nearly thrown off his legs. At once they both flew to her head, but she was a match for them. She went on plunging and kicking and rearing in a most desperate manner. At last she kicked right over the carriage pole and fell down.

York quickly sat down flat on her head to prevent her struggling. At the same time he called out, "Unbuckle the black horse! Run for the winch and unscrew the carriage pole. Cut the trace here, somebody, if you can't unhitch it."

The groom soon set me free from Ginger and the carriage, and led me back to my box. He turned me in just as I was and ran back to

York. I was very miserable and felt much inclined to kick the first person who came near me.

Before long, however, Ginger was led in by two grooms, a good deal knocked about and bruised. York came with her and gave his orders and then came to look at me. In a moment he let down my head.

"Confound these bearing reins!" he said to himself. "I thought we would have some trouble soon."

Ginger was never put in the carriage again. When she had recovered from her bruises, one of Lord W——'s younger sons said he would like to have her. He was sure she would make a good hunter.

As for me, I was obliged still to go in the carriage.

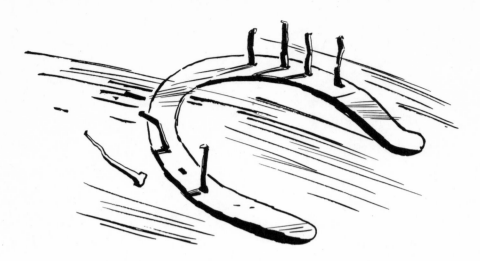

Ruined and Going Downhill

EARLY in the spring, Lord W—— and his family went up to London and took York with them. I and Ginger and some other horses were left at home for use, and Reuben Smith, the head groom, was left in charge.

No one more thoroughly understood his business than Reuben Smith did. When he was all right, there could not be a more faithful or valuable man. But he had one great fault, and that was the love of drink. He used to keep steady for weeks and months at a time. Then he would break out and have a "bout" of it, as York called it, and be a disgrace to himself and a nuisance to all who had to do with him. He was, however, so useful that York kept it from the Earl's knowledge.

It was now early in April, and the family was expected home some time in May. The light brougham was to be freshly done up, and it was arranged that Smith would drive to town in it and ride back. For this purpose, he took the saddle with him, and I was chosen for the journey.

We left the carriage at the maker's, and Smith rode me to the White Lion Inn and ordered the hostler to feed me well and have me ready for him at four o'clock. A nail in one of my front shoes had started to come loose as I came along, but the hostler did not notice it until about four o'clock. Smith did not come into the yard until five, and then he said he was not leaving till six as he had met some old friends. The man then told him of the nail and asked if he should have the shoe looked to.

"No," said Smith, "that will be all right till we get home."

He spoke in a very loud way, and I thought it unlike him not to see about the shoe, as he was generally very particular about loose nails in our shoes.

It was nearly nine o'clock before he called for me. He seemed in a very bad temper and was abusive to the hostler, though I could not imagine why.

"Have a care, Mr. Smith!" the landlord called from the door, but Smith answered angrily. Almost before we were out of town, he began to gallop, frequently giving me a sharp cut with his whip, though I was going at full speed. The moon had not yet risen, and it was very dark. Going over the stony roads at this pace, my shoe became looser, and when we were near the turnpike gate, it came off.

Beyond the turnpike was a long piece of road, upon which fresh stones had just been laid—large, sharp stones over which no horse could be driven quickly without danger. Over this road, with one shoe

gone, I was forced to gallop at my utmost speed. Of course my shoeless foot suffered dreadfully. The hoof was broken and split down to the very quick, and the inside was terribly cut by the sharpness of the stones.

This could not go on; the pain was too great. I stumbled and fell hard on both my knees. Smith was flung off by my fall, and since we had been going at such speed, he must have fallen with great force.

I soon recovered my feet and limped to the side of the road, where it was free from stones.

The moon had just risen above the hedge, and I could see Smith lying a few yards beyond me. He did not rise, and though he lay in the full moonlight, I could see no motion. I could do nothing for him nor myself, but oh! how I listened for the sound of a horse or wheels or footsteps. The road was not much used, and at this time of the night we might stay for hours before help came to us.

It must have been nearly midnight when I heard at a great distance the sound of a horse's trot. As the sound came nearer and nearer, I was sure I could recognize Ginger's step. I neighed loudly, and was overjoyed to hear an answering neigh from Ginger, and men's voices. They came slowly over the stones and stopped at the dark figure that lay on the ground.

One of the men jumped out and stooped down over it.

"It is Reuben!" he said. "And he does not stir."

The other man followed and bent over Smith. "He's dead," he said.

They raised him up, but there was no life so they laid him down again and came and looked at me. They soon saw my cut knees.

"Why, the horse has been down and thrown him! Who would have thought the black horse would have done that? Nobody thought he could fall. Reuben must have been lying here for hours. Odd, too, that the horse has not moved from the place."

Robert, the groom, tried to lead me forward. I made a step but almost fell again.

"Hello! He's bad in his foot as well as his knees. Look here—his hoof is all cut to pieces. He might well go down, poor fellow! I tell you what, Ned, I'm afraid it was the old thing again with Reuben. Just think of him riding a horse over these stones without a shoe! Why, he might as well have tried to ride him over the moon."

Then it was decided that Robert should lead me, and the other groom would take Reuben Smith's body home in the dogcart.

I shall never forget that night walk. It was more than three miles. Robert led me very slowly, and I limped and hobbled on as well as I could with great pain. I am sure Robert was sorry for me, for he often patted and encouraged me.

At last I reached my own box and had some corn. Robert wrapped up my knees in wet cloths. Then he tied up my foot in a bran poultice to draw out the heat and cleanse it before the horse doctor saw it in the morning. I managed to get myself down on the straw, and slept in spite of the pain.

The next day, after the horse doctor had examined my wounds, he said he was hoping the knee joints were not injured, but that I would never lose the scars.

When my knees were sufficiently healed, I was turned into a small meadow for a month or two. Though I enjoyed the liberty and the sweet grass, I missed Ginger very much.

I often neighed when I heard horses' feet passing in the road, but I seldom got an answer—till one morning the gate was opened and who should come in but dear old Ginger!

The man slipped off her halter and left her there. With a joyful whinny I trotted up to her. We were both glad to meet, but I soon found that it was not for our pleasure that she was brought to be with me. She had been ruined by hard riding, and was now turned out to see what rest would do. Lord George was young and would take no warning. He was a hard rider and would hunt whenever he could get the chance, without regard to his horse.

"And so," said Ginger, "here we are, ruined in the prime of our youth and strength. It is very hard."

We both felt that we were not what we had been, but that did not spoil the pleasure we had in each other's company. We did not gallop about as we once did, but we used to feed, and lie down together, and stand for hours under one of the shady lime trees with our heads close to each other. In this way we passed our time until the family returned from town.

One day the Earl came into the meadow, and York was with him. Seeing who it was, we stood still under our lime tree and let them come up to us. They examined us carefully. The Earl seemed much annoyed.

"There is three hundred pounds thrown away for no reason," said he. "But what I care most about is that these horses of my old friend, who thought they would find a good home with me, are ruined. The mare shall have a year's rest, and we shall see what that will do for her. But the black one must be sold. 'Tis a great pity, but I could not have knees like these in my stables."

After this they left us.

"They'll soon take you away," said Ginger, "and I shall lose the only friend I have, and most likely we shall never see each other again. 'Tis a hard world!"

About a week after this, Robert came into the field with a halter, which he slipped over my head, and led me away.

There was no leave-taking of Ginger. We neighed to each other as I was led off, and she trotted anxiously along by the hedge, calling to me as long as she could hear the sound of my feet.

A Horse Fair

No doubt a horse fair is a very amusing place to those who have nothing to lose. At any rate, there is plenty to see. Long strings of young horses out of the country, fresh from the marshes. Droves of little shaggy Welsh ponies no higher than Merrylegs. Hundreds of cart horses of all sorts, and a good many like myself, handsome and highbred, but come down through some accident or blemish, unsoundness of wind, or some other complaint.

There were some splendid animals quite in their prime and fit for anything. They were throwing out their legs and showing off their paces in high style as they were trotted out with a leading rein. But round in the background there were some very dejected-looking horses, so thin you could see all their ribs. These were sad sights for a horse to look upon, who knows not but he may come to the same fate.

I was put with two or three other strong, useful-looking horses, and a good many people came to look at us. The first thing was to pull my mouth open, then to look at my eyes, then feel all the way down my legs, and give me a hard feel of the skin, and then try my paces.

The gentlemen always turned from me when they saw my broken knees. But there was one man with whom I thought I would be happy, if he would buy me.

He was not a gentleman, nor yet one of the loud, flashy sort that called themselves so. He was rather a small man, but well made and quick in all his motions. I knew in a moment by the way he handled me that he was used to horses. He spoke gently, and his gray eyes had a kindly, cheery look.

He offered twenty-three pounds for me, but that was refused, and he walked away. I looked after him, but he was gone, and a very hard-looking, loud-voiced man came. I was dreadfully afraid he would get me, but he walked off. Later he came back and offered twenty-three pounds. The salesman had begun to think he would not get what he asked and might have to lower the price. A very close bargain was being driven, but just then the gray-eyed man came back again. I could not help reaching out my head toward him. He stroked my face kindly.

"Well, old chap," he said "I think we should suit each other. I'll give twenty-four for him."

"Say twenty-five and you shall have him."

"Twenty-four ten," said my friend in a very decided tone, "and not another sixpence—yes or no?"

"Sold," said the salesman, and the money was paid on the spot.

My new master took my halter and led me out of the fair to an inn, where he had a saddle and bridle ready. He gave me a good feed of oats and stood by while I ate it. Half an hour later, we were on our way to London. In the twilight we reached the great city. The gas lamps were already lighted. There were streets to the right and streets to the left, and streets crossing each other for mile upon mile. I thought we would never come to the end of them. At last, we came to a long cabstand.

"Halloo!" cried a voice. "Have you got a good one?"

"I think so," replied my owner cheerfully.

"I wish you luck with him."

"Thank ye," he said and rode on. We soon turned into a narrow street, with rather poor-looking houses on one side and what seemed to be coach houses and stables on the other.

My owner pulled up at one of the houses and whistled. The door flew open, and a young woman, followed by a little girl and boy, ran out. There was a very lively greeting as my rider dismounted.

"Now then, Harry, my boy, open the gates, and Mother will bring us the lantern."

The next minute they were all standing around me in a small stable yard.

"Is he gentle, Father?"

"Yes, Dolly, as gentle as your own kitten. Come and pat him."

At once the little hand was patting all over my shoulder without fear. How good it felt!

"Let me get him a bran mash while you rub him down," said the mother.

"Do, Polly, it's just what he wants, and I know you've got a beautiful mash ready for me."

"Sausage dumpling and apple turnover," shouted the boy, which set them all laughing. I was led into a comfortable, clean-smelling stall with plenty of dry straw. And after a fine supper I lay down, thinking I was going to be happy.

A London Cab Horse

MY NEW master's name was Jeremiah Barker, but as everyone called him Jerry, I shall do the same. Polly, his wife, was a tidy little woman, with smooth dark hair, dark eyes, and a merry little mouth. The boy was nearly twelve years old, a tall, frank, good-tempered lad. And little Dolly was her mother over again, at eight years old.

They were all wonderfully fond of each other. I never knew such a happy, merry family. Jerry had a cab of his own, and two horses which he drove and attended to himself. His other horse was a tall, white, large-boned animal called Captain. He was old now, but when he was young, he must have been splendid. He told me that in his early youth he went to the Crimean War. He belonged to an officer in the cavalry and used to lead the regiment until his master was killed.

The next morning, when I was well groomed, Polly and Dolly came into the yard to see me and make friends. Polly brought me a slice of apple, and Dolly a piece of bread, and made as much of me as if I had been the "Black Beauty" of other days. It was a great treat to be petted again and talked to in a gentle voice, and I let them see as well as I could that I wished to be friendly.

"We'll call him Jack," said Jerry, "after the old one—shall we, Polly?"

"Do," she said, "for I like to keep a good name going."

Captain went out in the cab all the morning. Harry came in after school to feed me and give me water. In the afternoon I was put into the cab. Jerry put on my collar and bridle just as carefully as if he had been John Manly all over again. There was no bearing rein, no curb—nothing but a plain ring snaffle. What a blessing that was!

After driving through the side street, we came to the large cab-stand we had passed the night before. On one side of this wide street were high houses, and on the other was an old church and churchyard surrounded by an iron railing. Along this side a number of cabs were drawn up, waiting for passengers. We pulled up in the rank at the back of the last cab. Two or three of the men came around to look at me.

"Very good for a funeral," said one. "Too smart-looking," said another, shaking his head in a very wise way. "You'll find something wrong with him one of these days."

"Well," said Jerry pleasantly, "I suppose I need not find it out till it finds me out, eh? And if so, I'll keep up my spirits a little longer."

The first week of my life as a cab horse was very trying. I had never been used to London, and the noise, the hurry, the crowds of horses, carts, and carriages that I had to make my way through made me feel anxious. But I soon found that I could perfectly trust my driver, and then I made myself easy and got used to it. In a short time my master and I understood each other as well as horse and man can.

I never knew a better man than my new master. He was kind and good, and as strong for the right as John Manly. He could not bear careless loitering and waste of time. Nothing was so near making him angry as to find people, who were always late, wanting a cab horse to be driven hard to make up for their idleness.

One day, two wild-looking young men came out of a tavern and called Jerry.

"Here, cabby! Look sharp, we are rather late. Put on the steam and take us to Victoria Station for the one o'clock train. You shall have a shilling extra."

"I shall take you at the regular pace, gentlemen. Shillings don't pay for putting on the steam like that."

Another cab was standing next to ours. The cabby flung open the door and said, "I'm your man, gentlemen. My horse will get you there all right."

As they set off at a great pace, Jerry patted me on the neck. "No, Jack, a shilling would not pay for that sort of thing, would it, old boy?"

One Sunday morning, Jerry was cleaning me in the yard, when Polly came to us, looking very full of news.

"What is it?" said Jerry.

"Well, my dear," she said, "poor Dinah Brown has just had a letter to say that her mother is dangerously ill and she must come right away if she wishes to see her alive. The place is out in the country, and if she takes the train she would still have more than four miles to walk. She wants to know if you would take her in the cab, and she promises to pay you as soon as she gets the money."

"Tut, tut, we'll see about that. It's not the money I'm thinking about, but of losing our Sunday. The horses are tired, and I'm tired too—that's where it pinches."

"It pinches all round, for that matter," said Polly. "For it's only half Sunday without you. But you know we should do to other people as we would like them to do to us. And I know very well what I should like if my mother was dying."

"Why, Polly, you are as good as the minister, and so, as I've had my Sunday sermon early today, tell Dinah I'll be ready for her at ten. And ask Butcher Braydon if he would lend me his light trap. He never uses it on Sunday, and it would make a wonderful difference to the horse."

Away she went, and soon returned, saying he could have the trap and welcome.

"All right," said he. "Now put me up a bit of bread and cheese, and I'll be back in the afternoon as soon as I can."

At ten o'clock we started. It was a fine May day, and as soon as we were out of the town, the sweet air, the smell of the fresh grass, and the soft country roads were as pleasant as they used to be, and I began to feel quite fresh.

Dinah's family lived in a small farmhouse close by a meadow with some fine shady trees. There were two cows feeding in it. A young brother of Dinah's offered to tie me up in a cowshed and invited Jerry to come into the house for dinner.

"If your cows would not be offended," said Jerry, "there is nothing my horse would like so much as an hour or two in your beautiful meadow. It would be a rare treat for him, and for me, too, as I have brought some dinner with me."

"Do, and welcome," said the young man.

When my harness was taken off, I did not know what to do first—whether to eat grass, or roll over on my back, or lie down and rest, or have a gallop across the meadow out of sheer joy at being free. And so I did all by turns.

Jerry seemed to be quite as happy as I was. He sat down by a bank under a shady tree, and listened to the birds and even sang. He then ate his bread and cheese and gave me a good feed of the oats he had brought along. The time seemed all too short—I had not been in a field since I left poor Ginger at Earlshall. We came home gently, and Jerry's first words were, as we came into the yard, "Well, Polly, I have not lost my Sunday after all, for the birds were singing hymns in every bush, and I joined in the service. And as for Jack, he was like a young colt."

Jerry's New Year

THE WINTER came in early that year, with a great deal of cold and wet. There was snow, sleet, or rain almost every day for weeks, changing only for keen winds or sharp frosts. The horses all felt it very much. When it is a dry cold, a couple of good thick blankets will keep the warmth in us. But when it is soaking rain, they soon get wet through.

One day, while our cab was parked outside one of the parks, a shabby old cab drove up beside ours. The horse was an old worn-out chestnut, with an ill-kept coat and bones that showed plainly through it. I had been eating some hay, and the wind blew a bit of it that way. The poor creature put out her long, thin neck and picked it up, and then turned round and looked for more. There was a hopeless look in the dull eye, and then, as I was trying to think where I had seen that horse before, she looked full at me and said:

"Black Beauty, is that you?"

It was Ginger! But how changed! The beautifully arched and glossy neck was now straight and lank. The face that was once so full of spirit and life was now full of suffering. And I could tell by her frequent cough how bad her wind was.

I sidled up to her a step or two so that we might have a quiet talk. It was a sad tale she had to tell. After a rest at Earlshall, she was sold and for a while got along very well. But the old strain returned, and she was again sold. In this way, she changed hands several times, always getting lower down.

"And so at last," said she, "I was bought by a man who rents out cabs and horses. The man who hires me has to pay a lot of money to the owner, so it's all week round and round, with never a Sunday rest."

"You used to stand up for yourself if you were ill-used," I said.

"Ah," she said, "I did once, but it's no use. Men are strongest, and if they are cruel and have no feeling, there is nothing we can do but bear it to the end. I wish I was dead."

I was very much troubled and I put my nose up to hers, but I could say nothing to comfort her. Soon her driver came up, and with a tug at her mouth, backed her out of the line and drove off. I felt very sad indeed.

A few days after this, a cart with a dead horse in it passed our cabstand. It was a chestnut horse with a long, thin neck. I saw a white streak down the forehead. I believe it was Ginger. I hoped it was, for then her troubles would be over.

It was now Christmas week, and we had a great deal of late work. Christmas and the New Year are very merry times for some people. But for cabmen and cabmen's horses it is no holiday. Sometimes driver and horse have to wait for hours in the rain or frost, shivering with cold, while the people within are dancing the night away.

On the evening of the New Year, we took two gentlemen to a house in the West End. We were told to come for them at eleven. As the clock struck eleven, we were at the door, for Jerry was always punctual. The clock struck the quarters and then struck twelve, but the door did not open.

It had grown very cold and there was no shelter. Jerry got off his box and came and pulled my blankets a little more over my neck. Then he walked up and down, stamping his feet. He began to beat his arms, but that set him coughing, so he opened the cab door and sat at the bottom, and was a little sheltered.

At quarter past one, the door opened and the two gentlemen came out. They got into the cab without a word and told Jerry where to drive —an address two miles away. My legs were numb with cold, and I thought I was going to stumble.

At last we got home. Jerry could hardly speak, and his cough was dreadful. Polly opened the door and held the lantern for him.

"Can't I do something?" she asked.

"Yes, get Jack something warm, and then boil me some gruel." This was said in a hoarse whisper. He could hardly get his breath, but he gave me a rubdown as usual and even brought extra straw for my bed. Polly brought me a warm mash, and then they locked the door.

It was late the next morning before anyone came, and then it was only Harry and Dolly. Harry cleaned and fed us, and swept out the stalls, but he neither whistled nor sang, and Dolly was crying. I could gather from what they said that Jerry was dangerously ill. So two days passed, and there was great trouble indoors. On the third morning, when one of the other cabmen came to inquire about Jerry, Harry was smiling.

"Father is better," he said. "Mother hopes he will get well."

Jerry grew steadily better, but the doctor said that he must never go back to cab work again.

One day Dolly came running into the stable where Harry was brushing me. "Who lives at Fairstowe, Harry?" she asked. "Mother has a letter from there. She seems so glad and ran upstairs to Father with it."

"Don't you know? That's Mrs.

Fowler's place — Mother's old mistress," Harry said. "Mother wrote her last week. Run and see what she said, Dolly."

In a few minutes Dolly came dancing back into the stable.

"Oh, Harry, there never was anything so beautiful! Mrs. Fowler says we are all to go and live near her. There is a cottage that will just suit us, and a garden and a henhouse, and everything! And her coachman is leaving in the spring, and then Father will take his place!"

It was quickly settled that as soon as Jerry was well enough, they would move to the country, and that the cab and horses would be sold as soon as possible.

The day came for going away. Jerry had not been allowed to go out yet, and I never saw my dear master after that New Year's Eve. Polly and the children came to bid me good-by.

"Poor old Jack! Dear old Jack! I wish we could take you with us," Polly said, and she put her face close to my neck and kissed me. Dolly was crying and kissed me, too. Harry stroked me, but said nothing. He seemed very said. And so I was led away to my new place.

Hard Times

I was sold to a corn dealer, whom Jerry knew, and with him he thought I would have good food and fair work. In the first he was quite right. And if my new master had been there all the time, I do not think I would have been overloaded. But there was a foreman who was always hurrying and driving everyone, and no horse can stand up against overloading. I was getting so worn out from this cause that a younger horse was bought in my place, and I was then sold to a large cab owner.

His name was Nicholas Skinner, and he had black eyes, a hard mouth, and a harsh voice. He was hard on the men and the men were hard on the horses. In this place we had no Sunday rest, and it was in the heat of summer.

My driver had a cruel whip with something so sharp at the end of it that it sometimes drew blood. My life was now so utterly wretched that I wished I might, like Ginger, drop down dead at my work. One day my wish very nearly came to pass.

We picked up an unusually heavy load of luggage and passengers from the railroad station, and I had had neither food nor rest since the morning. I did my best and got along fairly well till we came to Ludgate Hill. Then, in a single moment—I cannot tell how—my feet slipped from under me, and I fell heavily to the ground on my side. I lay perfectly still; indeed, I had no power to move, and I thought now I was going to die. I heard a sort of confusion around me, but I did not even open my eyes. I could only draw a gasping breath now and then.

I cannot tell how long I lay there, but I felt cold water thrown over my head, and some liquid was poured into my mouth, and something was covered over me. I found my strength coming back, and a kind-voiced man was patting me and encouraging me to rise. After one or two attempts, I staggered to my feet and was gently led to some stables that were close by. Skinner came with a horse doctor to look at me.

"This is a case of overwork, more than disease," the horse doctor said. "There is now not an ounce of strength in him."

"That sort of thing don't suit my business," Skinner grumbled. "My plan is to work 'em as long as they'll go, and then sell 'em for what they'll fetch."

"There is a sale of horses coming off in about ten days," the horse doctor told him. "If you rest him and feed him up, he may pick up. Then you may get more than his skin is worth, at any rate."

Upon this advice, I had ten days of perfect rest, plenty of good oats, hay, bran mashes, with boiled linseed mixed in them. Those linseed mashes were delicious, and I began to think it might be better to live, after all. When I was taken to the sale, a few miles out of London, I held up my head and hoped for the best.

At this sale, of course, I found myself in company with the old, broken-down horses—some lame, some broken-winded, and some that I am sure it would have been merciful to shoot.

It was an anxious time. There was one tottering old man that took a liking to me and I to him, but I was not strong enough. Then I noticed an old gentleman coming, with a boy at his side. He looked like a farmer and had a kind, ruddy face and wore a broad-brimmed hat. I saw his eye rest on me. I still had a good mane and tail, which did something for my appearance. I pricked up my ears.

"There's a horse, Willie, that has known better days."

"Poor old fellow!" said the boy. "Do you think, Grandpapa, he ever was a carriage horse?"

"Oh, yes, my boy," said the farmer, coming closer. "There's a deal of breeding about that horse." He put out his hand and gave me a kind pat on the neck.

"Poor old fellow! Grandpapa, could you not buy him and make him young again as you did with Ladybird?"

"My dear boy, I can't make all old horses young. Besides, Ladybird was not so very old. She was run down and badly used."

"Well, Grandpapa, I don't believe this one is old. Look at his mane and tail. I wish you would look into his mouth, and then you could tell. And though he is thin, his eyes are not sunken like some old horses'."

The old gentleman laughed. "Bless the boy! He is as horsey as his old grandfather."

In the end, the boy had his way, and Mr. Thoroughgood, which was the farmer's name, bought me and took me back to his farm. He gave orders that I be given hay and oats every night and morning, and the run of the meadow during the day. "And you, Willie," said he, "must take care of him. I give him in charge to you."

The boy was proud of his charge and undertook it in all seriousness. Sometimes he brought his grandfather to see me, and he always looked closely at my legs.

"This is what we have to watch, Willie," he would say. "But he is improving so steadily that I think we will see some changes in the spring."

During the winter my legs improved so much that I began to feel quite young again. When spring came, Mr. Thoroughgood and Willie tried me in the phaeton and were well pleased with my paces.

"Oh, Grandpapa, I'm so glad you bought him!" Willie said.

"So am I, my boy, but he has you to thank more than me. We must now look for some quiet place where he will be appreciated."

My Last Home

ONE DAY during this summer the groom cleaned and dressed me with such extra care that I thought some new change must be at hand. Even the harness had added polish. Willie seemed half anxious, half merry, as he got into the cart with his grandfather.

"If the ladies take to him," said the old gentleman, "they'll be suited and he'll be suited. We can try."

At the distance of two miles from the village, we came to a pretty house with a lawn and shrubbery, and a driveway up to the door. Willie rang the bell and asked if Miss Blomefield or her sisters were at home. Yes, they were. So, while Willie stayed with me, Mr. Thoroughgood went into the house. Soon he returned followed by three ladies. The very stately-looking one was the oldest sister. They all came and looked at me and asked questions.

Mr. Thoroughgood suggested they take me on trial and let their coachman see what he thought of me.

"You have always been such a good adviser to us about our horses," said the stately lady, "that we will accept your offer with thanks."

The next morning a smart-looking young man came for me. I was led home, placed in a comfortable stable, fed, and left to myself. The next day, when my groom was cleaning my face, he said:

"That is just like the star that Black Beauty had. He is much the same height, too. I wonder where he is now."

A little further on, he came to the place in my neck where I had been bled, and where a little knot was left in the skin. He almost started, and began to look me over carefully, talking to himself.

"White star in the forehead, one white foot on the off side, this little knot just in that place"—then looking at the middle of my back—"and as I am alive, there is that little patch of white hair that John used to call 'Beauty's threepenny bit.' It *must* be Black Beauty! Why, Beauty! Beauty! Do you know me? Little Joe Green that almost killed you?"

I could not say that I remembered him, for now he was a fine grown young fellow. But I was sure he knew me and was Joe Green. I put my nose up to him and tried to say that we were friends.

"Give you a fair trial! I should think so indeed! I wonder who the rascal was who broke your knees, my old Beauty! Well, it won't be my fault if you don't have good times now."

In the afternoon I was put into a low carriage and brought to the door. The youngest sister, Miss Ellen, was going to try me, and Green went with her. I soon found that she was a good driver, and she seemed pleased with my paces. I heard Joe telling her he was sure I was Squire Gordon's old Black Beauty.

When we returned, the other sisters came out to hear how I had behaved myself. Miss Ellen told them what she had just heard, and said:

"I shall certainly write to Mrs. Gordon, and tell her that her favorite horse has come to us. How pleased she will be!"

I have now lived in this happy place a whole year. Joe is the best and kindest of grooms. My work is easy and pleasant, and I feel my strength and spirits all coming back again.

Willie always speaks to me when he can, and treats me as his special friend. My ladies have promised that I shall never be sold, and so I have nothing to fear. And here my story ends. My troubles are all over, and I am at home.